Mack and Muck!

For Appoline . S . B

First published in paperback in Great Britain
by HarperCollins Children's Books in 2013

13 5 7 9 10 8 6 4 2

iSBN: 978-0-00-742530-3

HarperCollins Children's Books is a division of HarperCollins Publishers Ltd.

Text and illustrations copyright © Sebastien Braun 2013

Visit our website at: www.harpercollins.co.uk

Printed and bound in China

Mack and Muck!

by Sebastien Braun

HarperCollins *Children's Books*

Brrm!

Brrm!

Brrm!

This is Mack. Hello, Mack!

He is a very happy little tractor.

Every day Mack is busy on the farm:

ploughing fields,

carrying heavy loads,

watering crops,

and, best of all, baling hay...

all by himself.

One morning, just as Mack was getting up,
Beep the jeep dashed past.
"Come on, Mack," she called,
"the farmer's got a surprise!"

Mack followed Beep to the yard...

and found everyone gathered round a *new* tractor.

"Oh," sighed Beep. "Isn't he cute?"

"And so small!" said Harvey the combine harvester.

"Mack, this is Muck," announced the farmer. "He's come to live with us. Today I want you to teach him hay baling. And remember — he's only little."

Mack took Muck to the field and showed him how to roll the hay into big, round bales.

But Muck just scattered hay all over the place.

"You're not doing it right, Muck!" said Mack.
"Be kind," called out Beep, passing by.
"Muck's only just learning."

A little while later, Muck had filled the whole field with hay bales.

"Finished!" he said proudly.

Muck had only rolled one bale...
and it was *tiny*.

"Aren't you clever, Muck!" said Beep.

"B-b-but..." began Mack.
"Now, now," said Beep.
"This is Muck's first time."

Next Mack showed Muck how to lift
the bales to build a haystack.

Brrm!
Brrm!
Brrm!

"It's my turn now," said Muck.
"And I can do it *myself*!"

"OK!" said Mack. "But do it properly."

Muck's haystack soon
started to grow.

But as it got taller, it got
more wibbly...

and more wobbly,

until...

"Don't panic," called Mack,
"I'm coming!"

Carefully, Mack helped Muck
out from underneath the hay.
"I'm sorry," sniffed Muck.

"Don't worry," said Mack kindly.
"There's a first time for everything.
Let's try again!"

And so together, the two little tractors
got back to work, taking turns...

until the job was done.

Everyone on the farm came over to admire the giant stack of hay.
"Well done, Mack and Muck!" said the farmer.

And then they all paraded around
the farm in celebration.

Mack was so happy. Having someone new at the farm could be fun, after all!

"Thank you for helping me today," said Muck
as they made their way back to the barn.
"When I'm big, I want to be just like YOU!"

Soon Muck was fast asleep.

"There's room for everyone on our farm,"
Beep told Mack, "and Muck is so lucky to have
a big tractor like you to look after him."

Mack yawned happily...

Brrm!
Brrm!
Brrm!

"It's all in a day's work," he said.